Amusing Musings

Hilarious one-liners and deep thoughts for the offbeat sense of humor

By

J.J. Harlan

DEDICATION

To My Mother:

For still acknowledging that she's related to me despite
books like these. Thanks, Ma, I love you!

ACKNOWLEDGMENTS

I'm tremendously grateful to my loving wife for her unwavering support, and for not leaving me after I asked her, "Is this one funny?" for the ten-thousandth time.

Thanks for your purchase!
If you enjoy this book,
please leave an Amazon
review!

*Win a FREE
autographed book by
J.J. Harlan. New
winners selected
every month!*

jjharlanscifi@gmail.com

I just read a story about cannibals on a remote island that threw stranded sailors in a big pot and boiled them into soup. That's disgusting! Everybody knows people don't taste good unless they are properly sautéed.

*I*f cats could talk, I bet that when they cleaned themselves they'd never shut up about how good they taste.

*P*robably in the olden days, peasants who didn't have money for salt or pepper seasoned their food with sand instead. It was tough times for those peasants.

I *think it would be a good idea if scientists invented a new fruit. It should look like an orange, but "surprise," it tastes like a watermelon. Also, it screams when you peel it.*

If you're ever lost in the jungle, a good tip is to find a river and follow it. I think it's because it'll eventually lead to the sea or something. From there, you can signal a boat or swim to another country without jungles.

*I*t's strange how you can tell someone a funny joke six times and they still don't get it. And then, if you get a little excited, and tell the joke again, even louder, and you reach over the counter and shake the person because they still aren't laughing, it's not your fault if they begin to cry. They shouldn't throw you out of the bank for trying to tell a joke!

*H*ere's a tip if you ever get stuck in quicksand: don't struggle, you'll just sink faster. Instead, repeatedly clench your buttocks as quickly as possible to propel yourself up and out of the quicksand.

If you ever spend the night in a haunted mansion, be careful when you use the bathroom. That's where the pervert ghosts like to hang out.

*A*s I drove the locomotive full speed through the beautiful countryside, I tooted the train whistle and realized this might be the greatest day of my life.

Probably not so much for the conductor banging on the door, begging to be let back into the engine room.

If Martians landed in New York, I'm sure they'd be surprised at the number of hot dog stands in the city. You just don't find that many on Mars.

*W*hat is true love?
It's hearing your lover tell the same joke for the thousandth time and not stabbing them in the eye.

I bet when aliens abduct people to perform experiments on them, they probably make them sign a bunch of waivers first. An intergalactic malpractice suit could get pretty complicated.

*M*any people don't realize that "The Man" is actually Gunther Hammond who runs a convenience store in Iosha, Wisconsin.

If you ever catch a fish, and it just so happens to be a magic fish that will grant you any three wishes if you throw him back in the water, don't do it! Those talking fish are good eating.

If I was on a really boring date, and I wore a glass eye, I think popping it out and performing sleight-of-hand magic tricks with it could be a great way to liven up the evening.

Can you imagine what it must've been like for the last dinosaur that ever lived? I'm sure part of him was lonely, but there was also that part of him that was glad there were no more long lines for the bathrooms.

*I*t'd be a great idea to have firefighters wear holsters and carry guns like the police do. Of course, they wouldn't be real guns, just water pistols.

I *bet that dog heaven and cat hell are the same place.*

*W*henever you bring the word "milk" up in conversation, make sure you pause and clarify it's not "breastmilk" that you're talking about. Otherwise, people might be weirded out.

I *don't like to brag, but I'm a pretty good athlete. I'm especially good at those sports that involve penmanship or smelling things.*

*I*t boggles my mind how often people are rude in elevators. Every single time I press all the buttons at once, people get upset. C'mon folks, take the stairs if you're in such a hurry.

*T*wo good tips for boxers in a boxing match are: don't let your guard down, and always taunt your opponent in rhyme.

If you could go back in time and talk to the ancient Egyptians about modern life, I think it'd be the invention of the Cheeto that would fascinate them the most.

I *once read there are more insects living on the planet than people. Neat fact.*

It didn't specify which planet, so I can't speak to that.

There are two types of people in this world: those that enjoy eating in the nude, and those that kick you out of the restaurant when you're trying to do just that.

*I*n many ways, the
snail is the wisest of
creatures. "Why?" you ask.
If you were a snail, you
would understand.

I love Star Wars. Darth Vader is my favorite villain. An interesting fact is that at the bottom of his helmet was a little trap door, in case he wanted a lollipop but didn't feel like taking off his mask.

*E*veryone's impressed when my two-year-old nephew points to the sky and says "bird," but when I do it, they just stare at me. You people are impossible to please!

I *bet when the movie "Rocky" premiered, a lot of angry geologists demanded refunds in theaters.*

If you work as a Santa in the mall during Christmastime, and you're drunk, and you throw up on a kid sitting in your lap, I think you should tell him it was probably the milk and cookies he gave you last year.

*T*he Romans are remembered for their great contributions to the civilized world: mainly, paved roads, aqueducts, and the first Wal-Mart.

I asked Rebecca if she knew what clouds tasted like and she said they don't taste like anything, they're just made up of large collections of tiny ice crystals suspended in the atmosphere. Hahaha, sure honey. It's okay to admit you just don't know.

*W*hen you think about it, fishing is nothing more than a tug of war contest using a tiny rope.

I *think a good idea for a movie would be about a little boy learning to play the fiddle. All the other children laugh and tease him for taking fiddle lessons. Then, one day, his mother pulls an old dusty fiddle out of the attic and says, "This was your grandfather's magic fiddle. Whoever plays this fiddle will be the world's best fiddler." Then, all the other children will feel real bad about making fun of the little boy because now he was the world's best fiddler.*

Man, I hated those stupid fiddle lessons.

Calligraphy is a lost art nowadays. Also, sneezing with one's eyes open.

*O*ld people can easily be compared to an old book. On the outside, they might look plain and boring, but when you take the time and look inside them, you probably learn a lot of things you never knew. Things you don't care about and that are pretty boring. Instead of wasting your time with the "book," you probably want to watch TV or something.

*I*f you're making a cake, and the recipe ever calls for a cup of "milk," it's most likely referring to cow's milk. Trust me on this one.

If I could be any animal, I'd be a bird. You might think it's because they can fly, but that's not the reason. It's because nobody looks at them funny when they're eating worms.

*O*ne way you can find out the time of day is to use the sun. If you stare at it long enough, you won't be able to see anymore. As you stumble around, bumping into things because you're blind now, someone may come and offer you help. When they do, ask them if they know what time it is.

I'm sure the first maps were nothing more than a paper with squiggly dotted lines and a "You are here" written on it.

If you ever find yourself hard at work building a diabolical giant robot to take over the world, make sure you take a break once in a while to get some fresh air and stretch your legs.

*T*he best kind of book is one that's written about a character with a problem, who then rises to meet the challenge, and finally overcomes it in the end. Also, it has a scratch-and-sniff page at the back.

A good life tip is to bring a stick of butter with you to bed every night. That way, if you wake up during the night and want some butter... BAM! It's right there!

*T*he saddest thing in the whole world is a crying clown who realizes that the humongous shoes he's wearing are actually the real size of his feet.

*W*hat is the smartest animal in the world?

If you said, "a dolphin," you'd be wrong. It's a chicken with its medical degree. Surprised? You shouldn't be. Medical school is hard.

*A*s a kid I loved going to Sunday school. I still remember my favorite stories about Jesus walking on water, feeding the crowds with fishes and loaves, and shooting laser beams out of his eyes.

*N*othing says "I love you" like a homemade handwritten card slipped under your lover's pillow while they're sleeping... despite that ridiculous restraining order.

*G*ive a man a fish, and he eats for a day. Teach a man to fish, and he becomes lazy and skips work to do it.

*W*hen I have my first kid I will call him "A". I'll name all my other children after a different letter of the alphabet. When "Z" is born, we'll stop having kids, because then I'd have to name them after numbers. Only a weirdo would name their child after a number.

*T*here is only one thing faster than the speed of light, and that is the run to the bathroom after two chili cheese dogs and Crazy Carl's Coaster.

*Y*ou'll never see a meteorite made out of cheese, and you know why? Cheese burns up too easily as it falls through our atmosphere.

*P*eople just can't seem to take compliments anymore. Like the lady at the grocery store pushing a baby stroller with a cute monkey in it.

*N*othing tastes sweeter than biting into ripe summer strawberries. Also, licking the handlebar of the mechanical car ride at Chuck E. Cheese.

*T*he three most challenging moves to master in Kung-Fu are "the dancing tiger," "the hidden dragon," and "the barking chihuahua."

*I*t's said Breakfast is the most important meal of the day, but how do we know that? Of course, Breakfast is going to say it's the most important, but you've got to remember this: Breakfast can be a liar.

*H*ere's a good way to get out of a speeding ticket: If a police officer stops you and asks why you were speeding, tell him you work for the fire department and are on your way to a terrible fire. Then look at his name tag, repeat his last name, and say, "Omigosh! You have the same last name as the people that own the house on fire!" Then the cop will get real scared and you can say, "Hurry, I'll meet you there!" Then, when he jumps in his car and takes off, you just go the other way.

Make sure though that he doesn't pull you over again the next day because, BOY, will you be in trouble!

*R*ebecca says I should take up a hobby. Uh, excuse me? What do you think I'm doing hiding in the bushes waiting for people to walk by?

*L*et's face it, burglars who leave behind thank-you notes are the most well-mannered and polite of criminals.

I *think it would be neat to be a Marine and let me tell you why. You wear a cool uniform, learn to drive a tank, and get to ring a bell while collecting change in a red bucket at Christmastime.*

*H*ow much wood could a woodchuck chuck if a woodchuck had a chainsaw?

*I*f you want to cheer people up at a funeral I think you should pretend to cry at first with everybody else. Then, when the priest starts talking, begin to laugh real hard. As he goes through the eulogy, just keep laughing as long and loud as you can. Pretty soon, everyone else will join in and start laughing too. Then, everyone will be cheered up. Just make sure you know all the people there, otherwise, they'll look at you like you're crazy.

I *bet a popular joke in medieval days was to sneak up behind a knight and stick a "kick me" sign on his armor with a magnet.*

*W*henever you go to a restaurant and have to wait for a table, tell the hostess your name is "Parpar." That way, when it's your turn, they'll call out: "Par-par-party of two."

I *think fortune cookies should be more realistic with their fortunes. "You shouldn't have eaten the cashew chicken," or "Your spouse is cheating on you," are probably accurate predictions for some of the people out there.*

If I were a nurse about to give a patient a shot, I think it'd be a funny joke to squirt a little bit into your mouth first and say, "Yup, it's not the poison!," then stick it into the patient.

*F*or kid vampires, pretty much the most embarrassing thing in the world is when all your friends already have their adult fangs, but you still have your baby nubbins. Hang in there little buddy, they'll come in one day.

*I*f you throw a boomerang, and it doesn't come back to you, it was probably just a stick, so, no big loss.

*H*ave you ever stuck a hotdog with ketchup and mustard on it in your pocket, smuggled it into the art museum, snacked on it while you're looking at the paintings, then, accidentally of course, sneeze some of the chewed-up dog on a nice painting because you took a bite with too much mustard on it? Yeah, me neither. Just asking.

I read somewhere that man is descended from monkeys. I don't think that's true, but if it is, it would explain a lot; especially about my Uncle Roger.

I don't think kidnappers should offer candy and toys to kids. They should offer something educational, like a calculator or a good book. Kids don't read enough nowadays.

When *you're a little kid and something traumatic happens, it sticks with you for the rest of your life. For instance, I'll never forget the time my mom robbed a bank. We walked in, went straight to the teller, and she said, "I want some money." The teller told her to fill out some slips and sign them. Then my mom pulled out her checkbook and wrote some stuff down then we waited as the teller counted it out. Then my mom walked out with the money. It's sad when children are exposed to criminal behavior like that.*

I *bet when a racehorse is done running a really hard race, it probably thinks to itself, "Yeah, it's Miller time." And then it's disappointed when all it gets is a carrot or an apple.*

*L*aundry tip: If you wear your underwear on the outside of your pants, you can go twice as long without having to wash them.

*W*e never see police using drug-sniffing pandas, probably because they're more susceptible to addiction problems.

I remember the time a Bigfoot ate our mailman. Luckily, my Uncle Roger and I caught the Bigfoot with a bear trap in our front yard before he could escape. The Bigfoot had put on our mailman's clothes and even stole his mailbag. He was screaming stuff like, "Let me go!" and "I am the mailman, you idiots!" Yep, some people called Uncle Roger "crazy," but I called him a "hero."

If I had a nickel for every time a child laughed, I'd probably try real hard to invent some sort of laugh-o-matic machine to use on them so I could get rich.

*L*ooking up at the stars, I realize what a magnificent universe we live in. It's huge. It's inspiring. Also, I'm pretty drunk right now and can't stand up.

*O*ne of the funniest jokes I've ever heard was about a monkey who steals an avocado and... wait, I mean a chicken gives an avocado to the monkey and says... Uh, I mean he... oh, never mind. It's sophisticated humor. You probably wouldn't appreciate it anyway.

I'm sure if you could understand spider language, you'd hear nothing but filthy swearing every time you walked into one of their webs.

A *s a child I loved to read comic books. I can still recall my favorite superhero: Mr. Amazing Super Captain Wonderpants—I can't remember his last name though... or was it 'Wonderpants'?*

I *used to love watching that show "The Muppets" with Kermit the Frog. Many people don't realize how many years it took to train those animals to talk.*

*I*sn't it funny to think about how some things began? Like, the first "bank" was probably just some guy who said to his friend, "Hey, I've got an idea. Give me all your money, and whenever you want some, you can ask me for it."

*I*f little boys are made
of snips and snails,
and little girls are made of
sugar and spice, then what
are dwarves made of?

**Thanks for your purchase!
If you enjoy this book,
please leave an Amazon
review!**

***Win a FREE
autographed book by
J.J. Harlan. New
winners selected
every month!***

jjharlanscifi@gmail.com

ABOUT THE AUTHOR

J.J. Harlan is a humorist and science fiction writer located in the magical, mystical land of the Pacific Northwest. When he's not drinking coffee and dreaming up strange worlds, he's hiking in the mountains with his wife, ever on the lookout for a UFO or a friendly Bigfoot.

If you enjoy humorous science fiction, please check out his other book: *Aliens and Androids* available at Amazon
https://www.amazon.com/dp/B07QCQJX65

Printed in Great Britain
by Amazon